The Magician's Horse
and other horse stories

Compiled by Vic Parker

Miles Kelly

First published in 2014 by Miles Kelly Publishing Ltd
Harding's Barn, Bardfield End Green, Thaxted, Essex, CM6 3PX, UK

2 4 6 8 10 9 7 5 3

Publishing Director Belinda Gallagher
Creative Director Jo Cowan
Editorial Director Rosie Neave
Senior Editor Claire Philip
Designer Rob Hale
Production Elizabeth Collins, Caroline Kelly
Reprographics Stephan Davis, Jennifer Cozens, Thom Allaway
Assets Lorraine King

ISBN 978-1-78209-457-9

Printed in China

British Library Cataloguing-in-Publication Data
A catalogue record for this book is available from the British Library

ACKNOWLEDGEMENTS
The publishers would like to thank the following artists who have contributed to this book:
Advocate Art: Simon Mendez (Cover)
Beehive Illustration: Gail Yerrill
The Bright Agency: Kirsteen Harris-Jones (inc. borders)

Made with paper from a sustainable forest

www.mileskelly.net
info@mileskelly.net

Contents

A Stormy Day

From *Black Beauty* by Anna Sewell

*In this extract from the famous Victorian novel, Black Beauty
is a young horse owned by a good, animal-loving master called
Squire Gordon. Here, he repays his master's kindness…*

O NE DAY LATE in the autumn my
master had to go on a long journey
for business. I was put into the dog-cart and
the coachman, John, drove it for my master.
I always liked to go in the dog-cart, it was
so light and the high wheels ran along so

pleasantly. The wind was high and it blew the leaves across the road in a shower. There had been a great deal of rain. Many of the meadows were under water and in one part of the low road the water was halfway up to my knees – but the bottom was level and my master drove gently, so it was no matter.

We went along till we came to the toll-gate and the low wooden bridge. The river was rather high, and in the middle of the bridge the water was nearly up to the woodwork and planks. There were substantial rails on each side, however, so people did not mind it. The man at the gate said he feared it would be a bad night.

We got to the town and I had a good feed from a nosebag while the master went about his business. He was engaged a long time, so we did not start for home till rather late in the afternoon. The wind was then much higher and I heard the master say to John that he had never been out in such a storm. I thought so too, as we went along the skirts of a wood, where the great branches were swaying about like twigs and the rushing sound was terrible.

"I wish we were well out of this wood," said my master.

"Yes, sir," said John, "it would be rather awkward if one of these branches came down upon us."

The words were scarcely out of his mouth when there was a groan and a crack and a splitting sound, and crashing down

among the other trees came an oak, torn up
by the roots. It fell right across the road just
before us. I will never say I was not
frightened, for I was. I reared up, but I did
not turn around or run away. John jumped
out and was in a moment at my head.

"That was a very close call," said my master. "What's to be done now?"

"We need to go back the way we came."

So back we went to the crossroads. By the time we got to the bridge it was nearly dark. We could just see that the water was over the middle of it, but as that happened sometimes when the floods were out, master did not stop. We were going along at a good pace, but the moment my feet touched the first part of the bridge I felt sure there was something wrong.

"Go on, Beauty," said my master, but I dared not stir.

"There's something wrong, sir," said John,

"Come on, Beauty, what's the matter?" Of course I could not tell him, but I knew very well that the bridge was not safe.

Just then the man at the toll-gate on the other side ran out of the house waving his hands around like a mad person.

"Hoy, hoy, hoy! Halloo! Stop!" he cried.

"What's the matter?" shouted my master anxiously.

"The bridge is broken in the middle and part of it is carried away, if you ride onto it you'll be into the river for sure."

"Thank goodness we didn't!" cried my master loudly.

"You Beauty!" said John, and he took the bridle and gently turned me round to the righthand road by the riverside.

The sun had been set for some time and the wind seemed to have lulled off after the furious blast that tore up the tree. It grew darker and darker, stiller and stiller.

I trotted quietly along, the wheels hardly making a sound on the soft road. For a good while neither my master nor John spoke, and then my master began talking in a serious voice.

They thought that if I had gone on as my master had wanted me to, the bridge would have most likely given way under us, and horse, chaise, master and man would have fallen into the river. As the current was flowing very strongly, and there was no light and no help at hand, it was more than likely we would have all have drowned.

My master said that God had given men reason by which they could find out things for themselves, but he had given animals knowledge that did not depend on reason, and that this was sometimes better, and they had often used this to save the human lives.

At last we came to the park gates and found the gardener looking out for us. He said that my mistress had been in a dreadful state as she feared some accident had happened. We saw a light at the hall-door and at the upper windows, and as we came up she ran out outside, saying, "Are you safe, my dear? Oh! I have been so anxious!"

And my master replied, "If Black Beauty had not been so wise we would have been carried down the river."

I heard no more, as they went into the house and John took me to the stable. Oh, what a good supper he gave me that night, a good bran mash and some crushed beans with my oats, and such a thick bed of straw! And I was glad of it, for I was tired.

The Magician's Horse

By Andrew Lang

ONCE UPON A TIME there was a king who had three sons. One day the three princes went hunting in a large forest that was quite far from the palace. After a time the youngest prince became separated from his brothers and he lost his way. The two other princes were very worried, but when night fell they had no choice but to return home without him.

For four long days the youngest prince wandered through the forest, sleeping on moss and living on roots and wild berries. On the morning of the fifth day, he came to a stately palace.

The prince entered the open door and wandered through the many rooms – they were completely deserted. At last he came to a great hall where a table was spread with dainty dishes and fine wines. The prince sat down and ate, but as soon as he put down his knife and fork the table disappeared from his sight!

This prince couldn't believe his eyes! But even though he continued his search

through all the rooms he could find no one
to speak to. At last, just as it was beginning
to get dark outside, he heard steps echoing
from somewhere in the palace, and then he
saw an old man coming towards him.

"What are you doing wandering about
my castle?" asked the old man.

The prince quickly replied, "I lost my
way, hunting in the forest. If you will take
me into your service, I will stay with you
and serve you faithfully."

"Very well," said the old man. "You will
have to keep the stove alight all day and
night. You can fetch the wood for it from
the forest, and you must look after the horse
in the stables. I will pay you a gold coin a
day, and you will always find the table in

the hall spread with food and wine."

The prince knew he was completely lost, and couldn't find his way home, so he entered the old man's service.

Though he did not know it, his master was a magician, and if the flame of the stove went out he would lose a great part of his power.

One day while the magician was out the prince was working in the stables, grooming the magician's horse, when to his great surprise it spoke to him!

"Come into my stall," it said. "Fetch my bridle and saddle and put them on me. Then take the bottle that is beside them – it contains an ointment that will make your hair shine like pure gold. Then pile all the wood you can gather together onto the stove."

The prince was very surprised to hear a talking horse, but he did what it told him. He put the bridle and saddle on the horse, used the oil to make his hair shine, and in a few minutes, there was such a big fire in the stove that the flames sprang up and set fire to the roof. The palace was burning!

The prince hurried back to the stables and the horse said to him, "Quickly, fetch me a looking-glass, a brush and a riding-whip, then climb on my back, and ride as fast as you can away from here."

The prince did as the horse bade him, and in a short time, the forest and all the country belonging to the magician lay far behind them.

In the meantime the magician returned to his palace, which he found in burning ruins, with his servant and his horse gone. Enraged, he instantly mounted another horse from his stables and set out in pursuit.

As the prince rode, the quick ears of the horse heard the sound of the magician coming after them. "Throw the looking-glass on the ground," said the horse. So the prince threw it and when the magician caught up, his horse stepped on the mirror.

Crash! Its foot went through the glass. There was nothing for the old man to do but go back with the horse to the stables and put new shoes on its feet.

When the prince had gone a great distance, the quick ears of the horse heard the sound of following feet once more. "Throw the brush on the ground," it said.

And so the prince threw it, and in an instant the brush was changed into such a thick wood that even a bird could not have flown through it. When the old magician came riding up to the wood he came suddenly to a stand-still – he wasn't able to advance a step into the thick tangle. There was nothing for the magician to do but to retrace his steps to fetch an axe, with which he returned and chopped a way through the wood.

Then once more the quick ears of the horse heard the sound of pursuing feet. "Throw down the whip," instructed the horse. And in the twinkling of an eye the whip was changed into a broad river.

When the old man reached the water he urged the horse into the river, but as the water mounted higher, the magic flame back at the palace that gave the magician all his power burned smaller and smaller, until, with a fizz, it went out, and the old man and the horse disappeared.

"Now," said the horse, "you may dismount. There is nothing more to fear, for the magician has gone. Beside that brook you will find a willow wand. Pick it up then strike the earth with it. The ground will open up, and you will see a door at your feet, which leads to a large stone hall. Take me into it – I will stay there but you must go to the gardens beyond, in the midst of which is a king's palace. When you get there you must ask to be taken into the king's service."

The horse also made the prince promise not to let anyone in the palace see his golden hair. So the prince bound a long scarf around it, like a turban, and did everything the horse had instructed him to do. He left the horse in the stone hall, then went into the palace garden and asked the royal gardener for a job.

From then on, the prince worked all day, and he enjoyed his new work. But whenever his food was given to him he only ate half of it – the rest he carried to the hall beside the brook, and gave it to the horse, who thanked him for his faithful friendship.

One evening, when they were sitting together in the stone hall, the horse said to him, "Tomorrow a large company of princes and great lords are coming to your king's palace, to woo his three daughters. They will all stand in a row in the courtyard of the palace, and the three princesses will come out.

Each will carry a diamond apple in her hand, which she will throw into the air. The man whose feet the apple falls at will be the

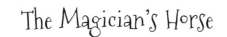

bridegroom of that princess. You must be close by, working in the garden. The apple of the youngest princess, who is the most beautiful, will roll past the wooers and stop in front of you. Pick it up at once and put it in your pocket."

The next day, everything happened just as the horse had said – the youngest princess threw her apple and it landed at

the prince's feet – but just as he stooped to pick it up, the scarf round his head slipped to one side, and the princess caught sight of his golden hair. From that very moment she loved him. The next day, all three sisters were married.

After the wedding, the youngest princess returned with her new husband, the prince, to the small hut in the garden where he lived, and they were very happy together.

After a few months, the king went away to war with a distant country. He was accompanied by the husbands of his two eldest daughters and his army. The king thought that the youngest daughter's husband wouldn't be of any use on the battlefield and must stay behind.

But when the prince heard that he had been left behind he hurried to the horse in the stone hall. The horse said to him, "Go into the next room and you will find a suit of armour and a sword. Put them on, and we will ride forth together to join the king."

The prince did as he was told, and when he had mounted the horse he looked so brave and handsome, that no one would have ever recognized him.

Then the horse bore the prince away swiftly to the battlefield. He fought so bravely and boldly with his sword that none could stand against him.

When the enemy saw the terrifying warrior in his glittering armour on his horse, they scattered and fled.

The king ran to thank the knight and saw that his leg was wounded. He hurried to bind it with his handkerchief, which had the royal crown embroidered upon it. Then to their astonishment, the horse rose up and bore the stranger out of their sight. It was all anyone in the kingdom could talk about, and news of the

hero travelled quickly. When the prince reached his hut he lay down on his bed and slept. His wife noticed that the handkerchief bound round his wounded leg was embroidered with the royal crown.

She ran straight to the palace and told the king. He followed her back to her house, and there the gardener lay asleep on his bed. The scarf had slipped off and his golden hair gleamed on the pillow. They all recognized the hero from the battlefield.

Then there was great celebrating throughout the land and the king rewarded his son-in-law with half of his kingdom, and he and his wife reigned happily over it for the rest of their days, with the wise horse as their companion.

The Princess on the Glass Hill

A retelling of an ancient Norwegian
fairytale by Sir George Webbe Dasent

ONCE UPON A TIME there was a man
who had a meadow, and in the
meadow there was a hay barn. But for the
last few years there had been very little hay,
because on every St John's night the crop
was eaten down to the very ground. It was
just as if a whole drove of sheep had been

there feeding on it overnight. The man grew weary of losing his hay so he told his three sons that one of them must go and sleep in the barn on the next St John's night and stop whatever was happening.

Well, the time came and the eldest son set off to the barn. He lay down to sleep, but there came a loud rumble and an earthquake, and the boy ran home in fear. The hay was eaten up again, just as it had been before.

The next St John's night, the middle son set off to try his luck. But once again there came a terrible earthquake, and he ran away frightened. All the hay was eaten up, just as before.

Next year it was Boots, the youngest

brother's turn. The other two laughed at him, saying Boots was useless and would have no more luck than they did.

Boots took no notice however, and went to the barn. That night there was an enormous earthquake. The lad thought the walls and roof were coming down on his head, but it soon passed, and all was still about him.

After a little while, he crept to the door and there outside stood a

horse feeding away. So big, and fat, and
grand a horse, Boots had never set eyes
on! By his side on the grass lay a saddle
and bridle, and a full set of armour for
a knight, made of gleaming brass.

'Ho, ho,' thought the lad, 'it's
you that eats up our hay? I'll
soon put a spoke in your wheel.'

So Boots threw the saddle
and bridle over the horse and it
became tame. He got on its
back and rode off to a secret
place, and there he kept the
horse. When he got home, his
brothers laughed and asked
how he had fared.

"Well," said Boots, "all I

can say is, I lay in the barn till the sun rose, and neither saw nor heard anything."

"A pretty story," said his brothers, and they trudged off to the meadow. But when the two reached it, there stood the grass as just as it had been overnight.

Well, the next St John's eve it was the same story over again. Boots went to the barn and everything happened just as it had the year before. This time, the horse that appeared was even finer and fatter than the first. By its side was a saddle and bridle and a full suit of silver armour. Well, the lad tamed and rode this horse, too, and took it to the hiding-place where he kept the first horse, and after that he went home.

"I suppose you'll tell us," said one of his

brothers, "there's a fine crop this year too, up in the hayfield."

"Well, so there is," said Boots, and his brothers couldn't believe their eyes when they saw he was telling the truth.

Now, when the third St John's eve came, Boots again went to the barn. The very same thing happened once more – and the horse that appeared was far, far bigger and fatter than the first two, with a saddle, bridle and armour of dazzling gold beside it. The boy again tamed it and rode off with it to the hiding-place where he kept the other two horses.

When he got home, his two brothers made fun of him again and said many spiteful things, but when they went to the field, there stood the grass as fine this time as it had been twice before.

Now, the king of the country where Boots lived had a daughter who was so lovely that anyone who set eyes on her fell head over heels in love. She lived in a palace next to which there was a high, high hill, made entirely of glass, as smooth and slippery as ice.

One day, the king announced that he would give half his kingdom and his daughter's hand in marriage to the man who could ride up to the top of the hill, to where the princess was to sit, and take three golden apples from her lap.

All the princes and knights who heard this came riding to the kingdom from all parts of the world. On the day of the trial, there was such a crowd of princes and knights under the glass hill that it made one's head whirl to look at them. Everyone else in the kingdom came to watch. The two elder brothers set off with the rest, telling Boots he wasn't allowed to go with them, and must stay at home.

Now when the two brothers came to the hill of glass, the knights and princes were all hard at it, riding their horses till they were exhausted. But it was no good, for as soon as the horses set foot on the hill, down they slipped. There wasn't one who could get a yard or two up — and no wonder, for the glass hill was smooth, slippery and very steep. At last all their horses were so weary that the knights had to give up trying.

The king was just thinking to himself that he would proclaim a new trial for the next day, to see if they would have better luck, when all at once a knight came riding up on a brave steed. The knight had brass armour, and the horse a brass bit in his mouth. He rode his horse towards the hill and went up about a third of the way easily, then turned his horse round and rode down again.

The princess thought she had never seen a knight so handsome, so she threw down one of the golden apples after him, and he caught it. But when the knight got to the bottom of the hill he rode off.

That evening the two brothers went

home and told Boots all about the wondrous knight. "I should so like to have seen them," said Boots.

Next day the brothers set off once more. They told to Boots stay at home.

When the brothers got to the hill of glass, all the

princes and knights were trying to ride up it again. But it was no good – they rode and slipped, just as before.

All of a sudden a new knight came riding up. His steed was even braver and finer than the horse ridden by the knight in brass. This knight was wearing silver armour, and his horse had a silver saddle and bridle. The knight rode straight at the hill and went up two-thirds of the way easily, before he wheeled his horse round and rode back down again.

The princess liked him even better than the knight in brass. She threw the second apple after him and he caught it. But after the knight reached the bottom of the hill, he rode off so fast. That evening the two brothers went home full of news about the incredible knight and his shining horse.

On the third day Boots begged to go and see the sight, but the two brothers wouldn't hear of it. When they got to the hill there was no one who could get so much as a yard up it. But at last came a knight riding on a steed so brave and fine that no one had ever seen its match.

The knight was wearing a suit of golden armour, and his horse had a golden saddle and bridle – so bright that sunbeams gleamed from them. He rode all the way to the top of the hill and took the third golden apple from the princess's lap before turning his horse and riding down and out of sight.

When the two brothers got home they

told Boots all about the dazzling knight.

The next day everyone in the kingdom was commanded to come before the king – and he asked if anyone had a golden apple.

"Yes, I have," said Boots, "here is the first, here is the second, and here is the third."

And with that he pulled all of the three golden apples out of his pocket! And at the same time he threw off his raggedy clothes and stood before them in the gleaming golden armour.

"Yes!" said the king. "You shall marry my daughter, and have half my kingdom."

So Boots married the princess and the bridal feast was so merry that the celebrations are still going on today.